Naming of God (in every religion)

Abdul Waheed

Naming of God (in every religion)

By- Abdul Waheed

SYMBOLS OF GOD

The symbols on this list are some of the most recognized and respected images that represent God in various religions and are used across the globe.

CROSS

ICHTHYS

CELTIC CROSS

ALPHA AND OMEGA

DHARMA WHEEL

MENORAH

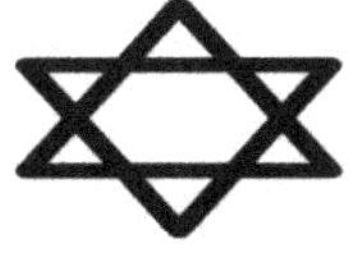

STAR OF DAVID

AHIMSA HAND

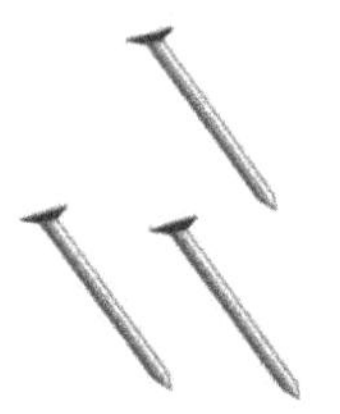

THREE NAILS OF THE CROSS

STAR AND CRESCENT

KHANDA

OM

YIN YANG

SWASTIKA

TORRI GATE

CERTIFICATE OF PUBLISHING

We're proud to present this certificate of publishing to

Abdul Waheed

for successfully publishing

NAMING OF GOD (IN EVERY RELIGION)

on 16-12-2022

"A writer's life and work are not a gift to mankind; they're a necessity"~ Toni Morrison

Dedication

This book is dedicated to the memory of my father Late Haji Ubairdur Rahman (Mutra) and younger brother Abdul Hameed, May Allah Ta'ala (God) rest their souls in peace,
"Aameen"

Table of contents

Preface

The word God is invented or named in different languages in each religion. To understand this one has to investigate the ancient inscriptions and history from which it is known. The concept that a person of any religion tells about God from his religion is so sure that this word is ancient than religion, it is adopted later, it is a part of some civilization (culture). By the way, many words of God have been used in the holy books of each religion, like in Islam there are 99 names, some people call them 101 as well. Similarly, there are many names of God in every religion of the world. Just as a name is given to identify a human being, in the same way God is named in the same regional language to identify him. As for the hair of atheists, they have got this word from the people of religion only. No matter how ancient an idol of any religion is, it is made into a form of one or the other human being, but God or God is a different thing, there is no idol of him. On this occasion, this book has been presented in front of you, please read it and gain your knowledge and if you have any information, please tell for the add.

Thank you .

Yours- Abdul Waheed, Barabanki, Uttar Pradesh, INDIA

Date- 15/12/2022

The name of God in ISLAM

There is no means of knowing what were the beliefs related to God in pre-Islamic Arab countries. The true picture about Islam cannot be obtained from Jewish and Christian sources. But, some inscriptions have been found in North and South Obia and there is evidence of some Greek writers. For example, fragments of the works of a Greek writer named Uranium Stephanus are preserved in Byzantium. On the basis of them, it can be said that like Job's 'Aloah', the word 'Ilah' is found in the writings of many Arabic tribes. The same word is used as a common noun in the Qur'an, such as 'the God of Moses' (4039) or 'I know no other god than myself' (28.38); ' A poet Vaidavi has also used the word 'Lah', but it must have been a form of Allah. 'Elah' was originally plural, like 'il', 'el' in Hebrew. This 'Ilah' became another plural of Elohem in the Bible. A similar word is found in the Arabic language from 'Allah' in the form of 'Illahum'. 'Ta'alatu ilaiya as ilaha' becomes a verb, which means to take refuge in God. Some people consider the meaning of this verb to be 'to serve'. The feminine of 'Ilah' is 'Ilah', which means the sun. The Greek Herodotus considers the sun to be synonymous with God. ,

Another word 'Rabb' is found in the Qur'an, which means 'Great' or 'Swami' (Master). By the way, it is singular in 'my Lord', 'your Lord'. But the plural is also found in the form of 'arvab'. In the

Jewish tradition comes sbbiono shel olam, which means 'lord of the world'. Similarly, in Arabic there is 'Rabb ul-'Alamin'. Thus, the use of 'Allah' or 'Al-Rabb' may be pre-Islamic. Syrian Christians use the word 'Allah' for their supreme deity. Saint Paul believes that Prophet 'Abdallah' (i.e. son of Allah) and the residents of Mecca were considered to be the family of Allah. The address 'Ya Allah' suggests that Allah must have been a name at some point. Alah in Hebrew and Ala in Arabic is a kind of adverb, which is used in the sense of one of the vows. The old word 'Ill' also comes for agreement. In the Safa inscriptions five times Allah comes with 'h' - 'so, o Allah' in the meaning of the same as 'so, o, allat' in the feminine gender. Here it seems that this word is used for a particular deity. Not for God alone. The word 'Laah' comes from the word 'Ilaih' which means to shine. In the inscriptions of South Arabia, the word 'Shayyim' (shelter-giver) appears.

God has also been called Vakil (trusted trustee) in the Qur'an. There is another word 'al-Rahman' in the Quran, which means 'merciful' or 'merciful'. Many liars also used this word for the Messiah, so it was abandoned. In pagan Armenian inscriptions it words are divine. The word 'Bismillah' is used between Allah and 'Al-Rahim', so that no one can misuse the word. In the liturgy, the old Arabic Ibadah meant 'the servitude of a slave to his master'. 'Aqfa is also in the sense of this service. Swami's service has also been called 'Hajar' - Huzoor, Mahzoor are his forms. Among the things that were offered to God, perfume and cloth were important. Even now a chadar is offered at the house of Allah. Sacrifices were offered in Mecca. Al-Uzza was smeared with blood (mukharshash). According to tradition gold, jewels etc. were also offered. 'Sadin' (a sheet of fine cloth) and treasures were offered. Another ism adh-metal in Arabic is the name of God's essence 'Allah' and on the other hand 'asm as-sifat' (attributes of God) are different names for them. When Muhammad Prophet called God 'Ar Rahman', then Ambu Jahl asked - 'When God has to be called by one name, then why this other name? On this in the Qur'an (7.179) there is this verse - God has many excellent titles, you call on him with them, and stay away from those who spoil the name of God. ' These spoilers were those people who make 'Allah' from 'Allah' and 'Al-Aziz into 'Al-Uzza'. According to the Qur'an (5319), it is a great sin to spoil such a name.

Tafsir of the Holy Qur'an

Tafsir Ibn Kathir

Surah yusuf 12, ayat 40

You worship nothing besides Him except names you have named, you and your fathers, for which God has sent down no authority. Judgment belongs only to God. He commanded that you should not worship anyone but God. Oh, that is the worthy religion, but most people do not know (40)

Then he explained to them that those whom they worship and call gods are simply ignorance on their part, and a designation on their own initiative that they received from their successors from their predecessors, and there is no basis for that from God. That is why he said: (God has not sent down any authority for it) meaning: an argument or a proof.

Then he told them that all rule, action, will, and dominion belong to God, and he commanded all of his servants not to worship anyone but him. Then he said: That is the upright religion, meaning: this is what I call you to in terms of monotheism of God and sincerity of work for Him. It is the upright religion, which God has commanded and revealed the proof for. And the proof that He loves and is pleased with is, "But most people do not know," meaning: That is why most of them were polytheists. (How many people will believe, even if you strive to be believers) [Yusuf: 103].

Ibn Jurayj said: Joseph changed their interpretation of the vision to this, because he knew that it was harmful to one of them, so he wanted to be busy.

Tafsir Ahsanul bayan

17,:110

Say: Call upon Allah as Allah, or as Rahman, by whatever name you call, all the good names belong to Him. Take (2).

110.1 As it has already been said that Allah's attribute name 'Rahman' or 'Rahim' was unknown to the polytheists of Makkah and it is mentioned in some sources that some polytheists used the blessed language of the Prophet (peace and blessings of Allah be upon him) or Rahman and When he heard the words of Rahim, he said that he is telling us to call on only one Allah and he himself is calling on two gods. On whom this verse was revealed (Ibn Kathir)

110.2 In his revelation, Hazrat Ibn Abbas narrates that the Messenger of Allah used to stay hidden in Makkah, and when he would lead his companions in prayer, he would raise his voice a little, and the polytheists would abuse the Qur'an and Allah after listening to the Qur'an. Allah the Exalted said, Do not raise your voice so high that the polytheists hear and curse the Qur'an, and do not lower your voice so low that even the Companions cannot hear. When it happened from Abu Bakr Siddiq, he was praying in a low voice, then when it was agreed to see Hazrat Umar also, he was praying in a loud voice. When you asked them both, Hazrat Abu Bakr Siddique said, "The one I was busy praying with, he was listening to my voice." Hazrat Umar replied that my aim was to awaken the Sutas and drive away the devil. He said to Siddique Akbar, "Raise your voice a little" and said to Hazrat Umar, "Keep your voice a little low." Hazrat Aisha says that this verse was revealed about prayer (Bukhari and Muslim, with reference to Fath al-Qadeer).

Aasr al-Tafsir Abu Bakr Al-Jazairi

Surah 12 Joseph, ayat 40

Abu Bakr al-Jaza'iri (b. 1921 AD)

(d. 1921 AD)

Oh, my companions in the prison: that is, my companions in the prison, and they are the two young men who are the king's food keeper and his drink holder.

Different lords: that is, gods who are dispersed here and there, that is, in their selves, attributes, and places.

 Without Him: that is, without God Almighty.

Except names: that is, just the name of a god, otherwise in reality it is not a god but rather an idol.

God has not sent down any authority for it: that is, God Almighty has not commanded that it be worshiped in any kind of worship.

So he gives his master wine to drink: that is, he gives his master, who is the king of the country, a drink of wine.

He is crucified: He is killed by being crucified on a stake, as is their custom of killing.

The matter is settled: that is, it has been concluded and decided upon.

He thought he had survived them: that is, he was certain that he was innocent.

Remember me before your Lord: that is, remember me before the King that I am unjustly imprisoned without a crime.

So Satan made him forget to mention his Lord: that is, Satan made Joseph forget the remembrance of his Lord Almighty.

Meaning of the verses:The noble context is still in the conversation about Joseph while he was in prison. The boys had previously interpreted their visions to Joseph, that is, they asked him to express them to them when they learned from him that he expresses visions. However, Joseph took advantage of the opportunity and started telling them about the reasons for his knowledge of interpreting visions and that he abandoned the religion of disbelief and his belief in God Almighty alone. In this, he is following the religion of his fathers, Abraham, Isaac, and Jacob, and that it is not appropriate for them to associate anything with God, and this is an exposure to what the people of the prison are doing, of associating others with God Almighty by worshiping idols. He continued his speech, calling to God Almighty, and he said what God Almighty told him in this context: {The companions of the prison are lords divided Better, or God, the One, the Supreme?" So he addressed his two companions, "O two companions of the prison, tell me and believe me: Lords, that is, gods, are dispersed here and there. This is an idol, and this is a planet, and this is a human being, and this is an animal, and this is such and such color, and this is such and such color." All creatures, and they had no answer except {Allah, the One, the Supreme.} The mind decrees this. Then he addressed all the people of the prison and said, "You worship nothing besides Him," that is, other than Allah, the One, the All-Mighty, "except names you have named.

Name of God in Zoroastrianism

The Iranians had brought many deities from the Indo-Iranian pantheon to their new country. Zarathushtra does not mention him in his prayers. It is not such a thing that it happened by chance; But Zarathushtra has done it intentionally. He was. He says that he recites words to his hearers, which were never heard before. All thinking and doing, whether human or divine, is done through the mind. It is knowledge or intelligence that builds, builds, guides. Therefore, adding intelligence to his divine imagination, he calls him

'Ahura Mazda'. It means 'lord wisdom' or 'wise lord'. The first word Ahur is of Indo-Iranian language and Mazda is of Iranian. All the deities that existed before this were nature symbol deities. But Ahura Mazda was not a nature god. In the Assyrian inscription of Sargon, a homonymous noun named Mazdaka occurs before 715 BC. In the inscription of Asmurbanipal, the word Asar Majas is found, which is the form of Ahura Mazda in the Assyrian language.

Zarathushtra uses the word 'Ahur Mazda' everywhere in his hymns and prayers. Both the words are used for the supreme authority. Among all the divine beings in Garonmana, the best is Ahura Mazda. He is not born. He is unique. He is such that there is nothing beyond Him, without Him or different from Him. He is the Supreme Being, from whom all things exist is possible. He is the most luminous, the highest and the most ancient. He is the best. No one is bigger than him. There is no one else equal to him. There is no one to challenge his greatness. He is the first and the best. He is perfect, omnipotent, He has authority over everything. He is supremely auspicious. He is immutable. He always remains the same. He will inspire everyone, make them move; But he himself is immovable. He is powerful, therefore he remains constant within all changes. In the battle of good and bad, he will decide who will win. He is the source of all happiness, therefore He is the subject of everyone's prayers. Everything happens through him. He is sovereign. He has many qualities. They are its main elements, that is, these qualities are not accidental in it. Ahura Mazda is the soul-form. He is the ultimate auspicious soul in his original form. Zarathushta for the first time in the world, in the history of religions, brought to mankind the conception of such a God, who is incomparable in his magnificence and who is incomparable in his excellence. He is superior to whatever supreme power was worshiped before him. He is beyond all the human like features in Arya and all the gods. Man knows abstract concepts with the help of words. Knows through physical images. Therefore Zarathushtra explains Ahura Mazda by giving the analogy of a human being. He speaks of his 'vision' or the words of his mouth. He distributes good and evil among humans with his 'hands'. He sits on his royal throne in the higher celestial world. Those who lead man towards virtue " "

-

He is ever present on the straight path. His clothing is the sky. All these descriptions should be taken as symbols. According to Gaia, Ahura Mazda can only be known through the mind's eye. The infinite can describe the infinite only through similes and metaphors. The house of Ahura Mazda is in the highest heaven above, above all the earth.

God is one but his names are many. What is the reason of this ? The scholars of Vedas know this secret but the common man does not know it. Most and many scholars of opinion-mutants also do not have accurate knowledge on this subject. Because of this, there is a state of confusion and confusion among his devotees and followers as well. Let us talk about God later, if we think about our name or names, then we find that people in the family and society know and call us by many names. We have a main name. In many people's homes, parents also keep a short name consisting of two or four letters to call them and call them by that. We have a main name for school and government services etc. which is different from the name we are called at home. In the same way, sons and daughters are also called by the name of mother-father, son-daughter or son-daughter. Some call us nephew, some call us nephew, some call us uncle and some call us uncle. Some also call us Mama ji or Mausa ji. Some call us Samadhi or father, friend, friend, Aryaji and many other names. These are many of our names, some are related to qualities, some are relative and some are related to nature and form, but our main name is the one which is entered or recorded in our school certificate or government records. Similarly, due to God's infinite qualities, deeds and nature, his devotees and followers also call him by many names according to their faith, devotion and feelings. Just as we have a personal and main name, like my name is Manmohan, similarly

Since

God also has a personal and main name "O 3 M". Other names are secondary, indicative of relation or telling and showing nature. Let us take the second rule of Aryasamaj, in which many names and qualities of God are discussed. The rule is that God is true, formless, almighty, just, kind, unborn, eternal, nirvikar, eternal, unique, universal, universal, omnipresent, ajar, immortal, fearless, eternal, holy and creator. He alone (God) is worthy of worship. ' If we consider the above mentioned names of God, then one name of God is Sachchidanand or Sachchidanand Swarup. This name is because God is Truth, Mind and Bliss. Because of these qualities, nature and form, God is called Sachchidanandswarup. This is the name of God with meaningful and true meanings. But the use of this name does not mean that Sachchidananda and O 3 M are separate Gods apart from the main name. Similarly other names of the same God are formless, almighty etc. The formless is his form. God being formless is called formless. In the same way a man is of low power and he can do only works with low power. Man cannot create sun, moon, earth, fire, air, water, form, sound etc. God has created these substances from the original nature with Satraj, Tama qualities. The creation of these substances is the work done by Apaurusheya or the Almighty Authority ie God. For this reason only the God named O 3 M is called formless and almighty. Similarly, the Arya Samaj

The other names mentioned in the above rules are also due to the qualities and nature of the same God, which are necessary so that while explaining it, the scholars can explain the true nature of God to the people with little knowledge. This also means that all the names of God in the Vedas and Vedic literature and they have been described as deities, they mean the qualities, actions and nature of God, including the creation of those substances by him and the things that happen from those substances. Because of the benefits he has been called and is called a deity. Why are earth, fire, air, sky, water etc all gods. It is not God but inert matter, but God created these substances from the original nature and created divine powers in them and all these substances have become our helpers in running our life smoothly. In the absence of earth, air and water etc., we cannot imagine to survive, let alone live a happy and blissful life. Therefore, due to the blessings of these non-living things on us, we call them by the name of gods. The meaning of God is to give the donation of your qualities to everyone. This air god is giving us the donation of life air. Because of expressing our gratitude towards them, we call them as deities. Similarly, for getting shelter from the earth, we express our gratitude by inculcating the feeling of mother earth, sons and ego of the earth. 60 percent and a little more of our body is water. It is because of this importance of water that we consider water as a deity i.e. a beneficent substance and express our gratitude towards it.

conservation, maintaining its cleanliness, saving it from pollution and making good use of it for living. Also know that there are two types of deities. Non-living deity and conscious deity. The non-living deities include the sun, moon, earth, fire, air, water, sky, food, medicine, vegetation, etc. whereas the conscious deities include the mother, father, teacher, mother cow, horse, king, judge and those who protect us from injustice etc. Protectors, humans etc. and all such beneficent creatures come. This benefactor is not God in spite of being a deity of root and animate matter and creature. Ishwar is not God but is called Mahadev because the favor that humans etc. all the creatures are getting from him, they do not get that much from any other deity created by him. Therefore, even though God has many names, He is all-pervasive, formless, omniscient and true blissful entity and is only one. We have to pray to his qualities to praise him and make our life happy and dreamy. Worship of God means thinking about his company and qualities is also essential and mandatory for us. By worshiping God, our evil and bad qualities, deeds and nature improve, we become equal to God and like him. If we look at the lives of true sages, sages, scholars and sages, then we can see in them the qualities corresponding to the divine qualities. In Ram, Krishna, Dayanand etc. also we see some qualities of God. Our great men became great by worshiping God. This is possible only because of worship. In this article, we have discussed many aspects of one God due to his qualities, actions, nature and relationships.

names have been discussed. We hope that the misconceptions that some of our readers have about this will be cleared. People will come to know that many Gods are not called by words with different names, but many qualities, deeds and benevolences of only one God are mentioned and highlighted.

The name of God in Hinduism

The name of God in Hinduism
is called Omkar in the Shrimadbhagwadgita as monosyllabic Brahman. In Mandukyopanishat, past, present or present and future have been said to be trikal-omkaratik only. Here the past element from Trikaal has also been called Omkar. The soul is Omkar from the point of view of letter and A, 3 and M form from the point of view of quantity. There is no quantity in the fourth pada and it is beyond behavior and non-dual. The meaning of this is that both the positive word Brahman and the Parabrahma past it are inseparable elements. Like Vedic literature, the glory of Omkar is found everywhere in Dharmashastra, Purana and Aagam literature. Similarly, the expression of devotion towards Omkar is seen everywhere in Buddhism and Jainism. The meaning of the word Pranav is - Prakarshennuyate stuyate anen iti, nauti stauti iti va pranavah. To make sense of Pranav, its analysis is necessary. Here, according to the process of famous Agamas, some guidance is given for the process of analysis. The names of the components of Omkar are-A, U, M, Bindu, Ardhchandra Rodhini, Naad, Nadant, Shakti, Vyapini or Mahashunya, Samana and Unmana. Of these, Akar, Ukar and Makar, these three are the readers of Brahma, Vishnu and Rudra, the editors of creation, status and destruction. By type, they are also readers of waking, dream and deep sleep and gross, subtle

and causal states. Bindu is the sign of Turiya dasha. The duration of pluth and long quantities are gradually shortened and finally in one quantity gets terminated. This is considered to be the pronunciation period of the Hasva vowel. The whole world is established on this one quantity. Pranav's condition is in this same quantity when he reaches the concentrated land from the neurotic land. In order to go from concentration to control, this M quantity is also differentiated and entered in half quantity. After that a distinction has to be made between the subtle and the more subtle quantities respectively. Bindu is semiquant. Beyond that there is a division of quantities in each level. After going to Samna Bhoomi, the matras become so subtle that it is not possible for any Yogi or Yogishwars to promote them, that is, the matras there actually become indivisible. It is preached by the Acharyas that in this place one should surrender the Matras and enter the Amatra Bhoomi. A little idea of this is found in the Mandukya Upanishad. Bindu is the form of the mind. Along with the division of matter, the mind becomes more and more subtle. Mind, time, imagination, deity and universe, nothing remains in the land of Amatra. This is called Unmani condition. There the Swayam Prakash Brahman remains constantly illumined. According to the Swachhand Tantra, a sequence of Omkar Sadhana is prevalent in the Yogi sect. According to him "A" is the dyotak of the entire gross world and Makara is the reader of the causal world situated above it. Because in Salil, the symbols of the three worlds are A, 3 and M. by the effect of vertical speed syllables get merged in Makara. After that, there is further speed of quantification. The movement towards M is called Anusvara movement. The reputation of Anuswar is in half the amount in Visargarup. When this happens, the door opens to go into the beyond. In fact, the movement of Amatra starts from the point itself.

יֵשׁוּעַ
Yeshua ha'Mashiach

Names of God in Judaism

Yahweh (or Yahweh) is the national deity of ancient Israel and the name of God in Judaism and Hebrew. The Jews believe that this name was first revealed by God to Moses. The word occurs several times in the Old Testament of the Bible, the scriptures of Christians and Jews. 4th century BC drachm (quarter shekel) coin from the Persian province of Yehud Medinata, possibly representing Yahweh seated on a winged and wheeled sun-throne The Hebrew script of the Jews can be written in Hebrew script with only consonants Can and not a laughing voice at all. So this word is made up of four consonants: (yod) (hai). (wao) (heh), or ain' means ya-h-v-h. People give it various pronunciations by inserting various vowels, such as Jehovah, Yahweh, Yahweh:, Jehova, etc. (since the ancient Hebrew language is lost). The Jews considered it a sin to use the name of God (Jehovah) unnecessarily, so this word was rarely spoken.

The more popular word was "Adonai" (meaning my Lord. In the
Old Testament/Hebrew scriptures of the Bible, the words "El" and

"Elohim" are also used for God, but surprisingly the Jews say that He is one God. But the word "Elohim" is plural!

Seven names of God in Judaism

The names of God that, once written, cannot be erased because of their holiness are the Tetragrammaton, Adonai, El, Elohim,[n 1] Shaddai, Tzevaot; some also include I Am that I Am. In addition, the name Jah—because it forms part of the Tetragrammaton—is similarly protected. The tanna Jose ben Halafta considered "Tzevaot" a common name in the second century and Rabbi Ishmael considered "Elohim" to be one. All other names, such as "Merciful", "Gracious" and "Faithful", merely represent attributes that are also common to human beings.

YHWH

Tetragrammaton, Yahweh, and Lord § Religion

Also abbreviated Jah, the most common name of God in the Hebrew Bible is the Tetragrammaton, יהוה, that is usually transcribed as YHWH. Hebrew script is an abjad, so that the letters in the name are normally consonants, usually expanded as Yahweh in English.

Modern Rabbinical Jewish culture judges it forbidden to pronounce this name. In prayers it is replaced by the word אֲדֹנָי (Adonai, Hebrew pronunciation: [adoˈnaj], lit. transl. My Lords, Pluralis majestatis taken as singular), and in discussion by HaShem 'The Name'. Nothing in the Torah explicitly prohibits speaking the name and the Book of Ruth shows it was being pronounced as late as the 5th century BCE.[n 2] Mark Sameth argues that only a pseudo name was pronounced, the four letters YHWH being a cryptogram which the priests of ancient Israel read in reverse as huhi, 'heshe', signifying a dual-gendered deity, as earlier theorized by Guillaume Postel (16th century) and Michelangelo Lanci [it] (19th century). It had ceased to be spoken aloud by at least the 3rd century BCE, during Second Temple Judaism. The Talmud relates, perhaps anecdotally, this began with the death of Simeon the Just. Vowel points began to be added to the Hebrew text only in the early medieval period. The Masoretic Text adds to the Tetragrammaton the vowel points of Adonai or Elohim (depending on the context), indicating that these are the words to be pronounced in place of the

Tetragrammaton (see Qere and Ketiv), as shown also by the subtle pronunciation changes when combined with a preposition or a conjunction. This is in contrast to Karaite Jews, who traditionally viewed pronouncing the Tetragrammaton as a mitzvah because the name appears some 6800 times throughout the Tanakh; though most modern Karaites, under pressure and seeking acceptance from mainstream Rabbinical Jews, now also use the term Adonai instead, and the Beta Israel, who pronounce the Tetragrammaton as Yahu, but also use the Geʿez term Igziabeher.

The Tetragrammaton appears in Genesis and occurs 6,828 times in total in the Biblia Hebraica Stuttgartensia edition of the Masoretic Text. It is thought to be an archaic third-person singular of the imperfective aspect[n 3] of the verb "to be" (i.e., "[He] is/was/will be"). This agrees with the passage in Exodus where God names himself as "I Will Be What I Will Be" using the first-person singular imperfective aspect, open to interpretation as present tense ("I am what I am"), future ("I shall be what I shall be"), or imperfect ("I used to be what I used to be").

Rabbinic Judaism teaches that the name is forbidden to all except the High Priest of Israel, who should only speak it in the Holy of Holies of the Temple in Jerusalem on Yom Kippur. He then pronounces the name "just as it is written." As each blessing was made, the people in the courtyard were to prostrate themselves completely as they heard it spoken aloud. As the Temple has not been rebuilt since its destruction in 70 CE, most modern Jews never pronounce YHWH but instead read אֲדֹנָי (Adonai, Hebrew pronunciation: [ʾăḏōnāy], lit. transl. My Lords, Pluralis majestatis taken as singular) during prayer and while reading the Torah and as HaShem ("The Name") at other times. Similarly, the Vulgate used Dominus ('The Lord') and most English translations of the Bible write "the LORD" for YHWH and "the LORD God", "the Lord GOD" or "the Sovereign LORD" for Adonai YHWH instead of transcribing the name. The Septuagint may have originally used the Hebrew letters themselves amid its Greek text, but there is no scholarly consensus on this point. All surviving Christian-era manuscripts use Kyrios (Κυριος, "Lord") or very occasionally Theos (Θεος, "God") to translate the many thousand occurrences of the Name. However, given the great preponderance of the anarthrous Kyrios solution for translating YHWH in the Septuagint and some disambiguation efforts by Christian-era copyists involving Kyrios (see especially scribal activity in Acts),

אֲדֹנָי (ăḏōnāy, lit. transl. My Lords, pluralis majestatis taken as singular) is the possessive form of adon ('Lord'), along with the first-person singular pronoun enclitic.[n 4] As with Elohim, Adonai's grammatical form is usually explained as a plural of majesty. In the Hebrew Bible, the word is nearly always used to refer to God (approximately 450 occurrences). As pronunciation of the Tetragrammaton came to be avoided in the Hellenistic period, Jews may have begun to drop the Tetragrammaton when presented alongside Adonai and subsequently to expand it to cover for the Tetragrammaton in the forms of spoken prayer and written scripture. Owing to the expansion of chumra (the idea of "building a fence around the Torah"), the word Adonai itself has come to be too holy to say for Orthodox Jews outside of prayer, leading to its replacement by HaShem ('The Name').

The singular forms adon and adoni ('my lord') are used in the Hebrew Bible as royal titles, as in the First Book of Samuel, and for distinguished persons. The Phoenicians used it as a title of Tammuz (the origin of the Greek Adonis). It is also used very occasionally in Hebrew texts to refer to God (e.g. Psalm 136:3.) Deuteronomy 10:17 has the proper name Yahweh alongside the superlative constructions "God of gods" (elōhê ha-elōhîm, literally, "the gods of gods") and "Lord of lords" (adōnê ha-adōnîm, "the lords of lords": כִּי

יְהוָה אֱלֹהֵיכֶם הוּא אֱלֹהֵי הָאֱלֹהִים וַאֲדֹנֵי הָאֲדֹנִים; KJV: "For the LORD your God is God of gods, and Lord of lords").

The final syllable of Adonai uses the vowel kamatz, rather than patach which would be expected from the Hebrew for 'my lord(s)'. Professor Yoel Elitzur explains this as a normal transformation when a Hebrew word becomes a name, giving as other examples Nathan, Yitzchak, and Yigal. As Adonai became the most common reverent substitute for the Tetragrammaton, it too became considered un-erasable due to its holiness. As such, most prayer books avoid spelling out the word Adonai, and instead write two yodhs (יְיָ) in its place.

The forms Adaunoi, Adoinoi, and Adonoi represent Ashkenazi Hebrew variant pronunciations of the word Adonai.

Elohim

A common name of God in the Hebrew Bible is Elohim (אלהים, ʼĕlōhīm), the plural of אֱלוֹהַּ (Eloah). When Elohim refers to God in the Hebrew Bible, singular verbs are used. The word is identical to elohim meaning gods and is cognate to the 'lhm found in Ugaritic, where it is used for the pantheon of Canaanite gods, the children of El and conventionally vocalized as "Elohim" although the original Ugaritic vowels are unknown. When the Hebrew Bible uses elohim not in reference to God, it is plural (for example, Exodus 20:2). There are a few other such uses in Hebrew, for example Behemoth. In Modern Hebrew, the singular word ba'alim ('owner') looks plural, but likewise takes a singular verb.

A number of scholars have traced the etymology to the Semitic root *yl, 'to be first, powerful', despite some difficulties with this view. Elohim is thus the plural construct 'powers'. Hebrew grammar allows for this form to mean "He is the Power (singular) over powers (plural)", just as the word Ba'alim means 'owner' (see above). "He is lord (singular) even over any of those things that he owns that are lordly (plural)".

Theologians who dispute this claim cite the hypothesis that plurals of majesty came about in more modern times. Richard Toporoski, a classics scholar, asserts that plurals of majesty first appeared in the reign of Diocletian (CE 284–305). Indeed, Gesenius states in his book Hebrew Grammar the following:

The Jewish grammarians call such plurals ... plur. virium or virtutum; later grammarians call them plur. excellentiae, magnitudinis, or plur. maiestaticus. This last name may have been suggested by the we used by kings when speaking of themselves (compare 1 Maccabees 10:19 and 11:31); and the plural used by God in Genesis 1:26 and 11:7; Isaiah 6:8 has been incorrectly explained in this way. It is, however, either communicative (including the attendant angels: so at all events in Isaiah 6:8 and Genesis 3:22), or according to others, an indication of the fullness of power and might implied. It is best explained as a plural of self-deliberation. The use of the plural as a form of respectful address is quite foreign to Hebrew.

Mark S. Smith has cited the use of plural as possible evidence to suggest an evolution in the formation of early Jewish conceptions of monotheism, wherein references to "the gods" (plural) in earlier accounts of verbal tradition became either interpreted as multiple aspects of a single monotheistic God at the time of writing, or subsumed under a form of monolatry, wherein the god(s) of a certain city would be accepted after the fact as a reference to the God of Israel and the plural deliberately dropped.

The plural form ending in -im can also be understood as denoting abstraction, as in the Hebrew words chayyim (חיים, 'life') or betulim (בתולים, 'virginity'). If understood this way, Elohim means 'divinity' or 'deity'. The word chayyim is similarly syntactically singular when used as a name but syntactically plural otherwise. In many of the passages in which elohim occurs in the Bible, it refers to non-Israelite deities, or in some instances to powerful men or judges, and even angels (Exodus 21:6, Psalms 8:5) as a simple plural in those instances.

Shaddai

El Shaddai

El Shaddai (שדי אל, 'el šaday, pronounced [ʃaˈdaj]) is one of the names of God in Judaism, with its etymology coming from the influence of the Ugaritic religion on modern Judaism. El Shaddai is conventionally translated as "God Almighty". While the translation of El as 'god' in Ugaritic/Canaanite languages is straightforward, the literal meaning of Shaddai is the subject of debate.

Tzevaot

For the Gnostic deity, Sabaoth (Gnosticism).

Tzevaot, Tzevaoth, Tsebaoth or Sabaoth (צבאות, ṣəḇāʾōṯ, [tsvaot] ⓘ, lit. "Armies"), usually translated "Hosts", appears in reference to armies or armed hosts of men but is not used as a divine epithet in the Torah, Joshua, or Judges. Starting in the Books of Samuel, the term "Lord of Hosts" appears hundreds of times throughout the Prophetic books, in Psalms, and in Chronicles.

The Hebrew word Sabaoth was also absorbed in Ancient Greek (σαβαωθ, sabaōth) and Latin (Sabaoth, with no declension). Tertullian and other patristics used it with the meaning of "Army of angels of God".

Ehyeh

Ehyeh asher ehyeh (אֶהְיֶה אֲשֶׁר אֶהְיֶה) is the first of three responses given to Moses when he asks for God's name in the Book of Exodus. The King James Version of the Bible translates the Hebrew as "I Am that I Am" and uses it as a proper name for God.

Ehyeh-Asher-Ehyeh

The word ehyeh is the first-person singular imperfect form of hayah, 'to be'. Biblical Hebrew does not distinguish between grammatical tenses. It has instead an aspectual system in which the imperfect denotes any actions that are not yet completed, Accordingly, Ehyeh asher ehyeh can be rendered in English not only as "I am that I am" but also as "I will be what I will be" or "I will be who I will be", or "I shall prove to be whatsoever I shall prove to be" or even "I will be because I will be". Other renderings include: Leeser, "I Will Be that I Will Be"; Rotherham, "I Will Become whatsoever I please", Greek, Ego eimi ho on (ἐγώ εἰμι ὁ ὤν), 'I am The Being' in the Septuagint, and Philo, and Revelation or, "I am The Existing One"; Latin, ego sum qui sum, "I am Who I am."

The word asher is a relative pronoun whose meaning depends on the immediate context, so that "that", "who", "which", or "where" are all possible translations of that word.

The name of God in Christianity

On the basis of the Bible, Christians believe that a man can attain the knowledge of God even on the strength of his intellect. Despite being incomplete, this knowledge is authentic. Christianity does not necessarily have any relation with any one philosophy, but as a result of historical circumstances,

Christian philosophers often propound theism by resorting to the philosophy of Plato or Aristotle. The existence of God is often proved on the basis of cause-effect relationship.

·I·N·R·I·

Names of God in Sikhism

In Sikhism, God is conceived of as the unity that permeates all of creation and beyond. This one Omkar resides within the entire creation as a symbol of the symbol. One who gives up his ego and meditates on that Oneness, is indescribable, but knowable and perceptible. The Sikh gurus have described God in many ways in their hymns included in Sikhism's holy scripture, the Guru Granth Sahib, but the oneness of the formless God is constantly emphasized. It is believed in Sikhism that the universe was created from a single word of God. When the universe was created, it resulted in a sound. The sound is noted in the first word in the Satguru Sri Guru Granth Sahib Ji, Ik Ongkar. The syllable "Oong" is the sound that was made during the creation of the universe. The transcendental God expressed himself in "Naam" and "Sabd" which created the world. "Naam" and "Sabad" are the creative and dynamic effects of God.

This symbol is known as *The Greatest Name* (of God). It is written in beautiful Arabic calligraphy and translates as 'The Glory of the Most Glorious'.

It is often seen in Bahá'í buildings and homes.

The Name of God in the Bahá'í

Faith Manifestations of God refer to divine attributes, which are creations of God created for the purpose of spiritual enlightenment on the physical plane of existence. In the Bahá'í view, all physical beings reflect at least one of these qualities, and the human spirit can potentially reflect all of them. The Bahá'í concept of God rejects all pantheistic, anthropomorphic and anthropomorphic beliefs about God.

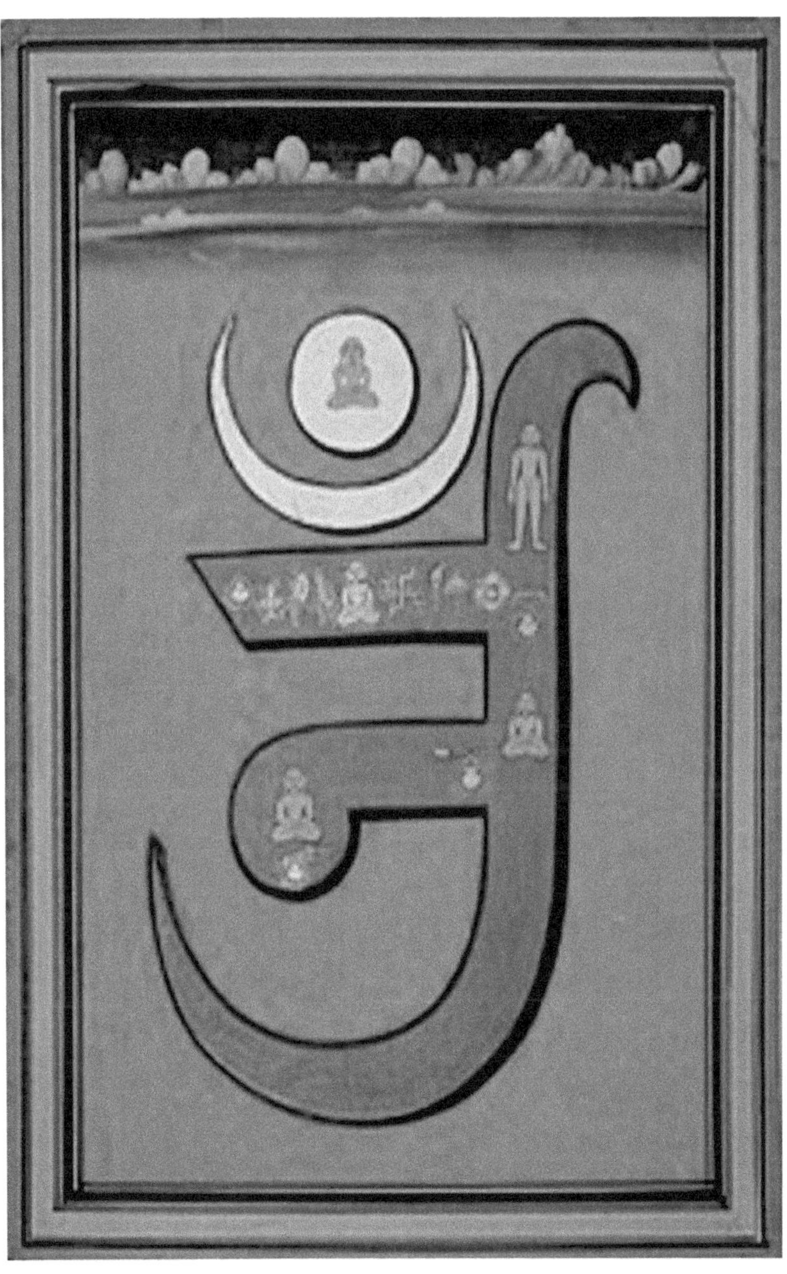

Name of God in Jainism

Lord Arihant (Kevali) and Siddha (liberated souls) are called in Jainism. Jainism rejects the concept of any creator god or power responsible for the manifestation, creation or maintenance of this universe. According to Jain philosophy, this world and its six substances (Jiva, Pudgal, Akasha, Kaal, Dharma, and Adharma) have always existed and will always exist. This universe is self-governing and runs on universal natural laws. According to Jain philosophy God, an immaterial object cannot create a concrete object (universe). Jain texts contain a detailed description of the devas (heavenly dwellers), but these beings are not seen as creators; They are also subject to miseries and like all other living beings, they end up dying at the end of their lifespan. According to Jainism no one created this universe. The gods and goddesses who are in heaven are there because of their good deeds and cannot be considered as God. These gods and goddesses are there for a certain time and they can also go to salvation after death only by becoming human beings. According to Jainism, the true nature of every soul is God and every soul has infinite vision, infinite power, infinite knowledge and infinite happiness. Due to the bondage of soul and karma, these qualities are not manifested. This state of soul can be attained through right philosophy, right knowledge, right character. The holder of these kingdoms is called God. a god, thus a free spirit

There is freedom from sorrow, rebirth, world, karma and finally - freedom from the body. This is called Nirvana or Moksha. These vitaragi gods are not worshiped by Jains for any favor or gift. The Vitaragi God is worshiped to destroy the Karmas and attain the Divine.

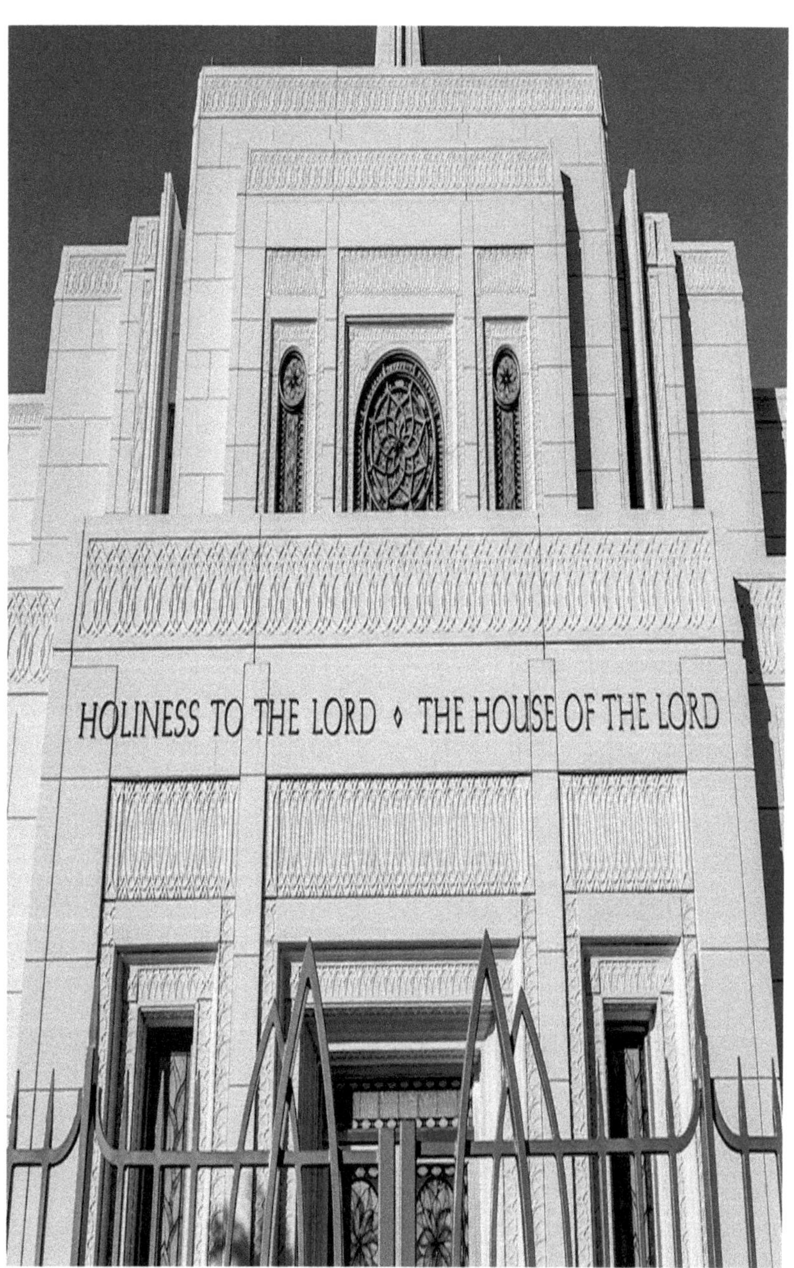
HOLINESS TO THE LORD ◊ THE HOUSE OF THE LORD

Name of God in Mormonism

In orthodox Mormonism, the term God generally refers to the Biblical God the Father, whom Latter-day Saints refer to as Elohim, and the term Godhead refers to a council of three distinct divine persons. It consists of God the Father, Jesus Christ His firstborn Son, whom Latter-day Saints refer to as Jehovah, and the Holy Spirit. Latter-day Saints believe that the Father, the Son, and the Holy Spirit are three distinct beings, and that the Father and Jesus have perfected, glorified physical bodies, while the Holy Spirit is one spirit without a physical body. Latter-day Saints also believe that there are other deities outside of divinity, such as Heavenly Mother—who is the wife of God the Father—and that faithful Latter-day Saints can attain divinity in the afterlife. The term Heavenly Parents is used collectively to refer to the divine partnership of Heavenly Father and Heavenly Mother. Joseph Smith taught that God was once a person on another planet before he was exalted as God. This concept differs from the traditional Christian Trinity in several ways, one of which is that Mormonism has not adopted or continued the Nicene Creed doctrine, that the Father, the Son, and the Holy Spirit are of the same substance or being.

Also, Mormonism teaches that the intelligence that resides in each human being is co-eternal with God. Mormons use the word omnipotent to describe God, and regard him as creator: they understand him as omnipotent and eternal but subject to eternal natural law that governs intelligence, justice, and the eternal nature of matter. governs (i.e. God organized the world but did not create it out of nothing. The Mormon concept of God also differs greatly from the Jewish tradition of ethical monotheism in which Elohim (78) is an entirely different concept. God's This description represents Mormon orthodoxy, which was formalized on the basis of earlier teachings in 1915. Other current and historical branches of Mormonism have adopted different views of God, such as the Adam–God doctrine and Trinitarianism.

The Name of God in the Gap

From the 1880s, Friedrich Nietzsche's Thus Spoke Zarathustra, Part Two, "On the Priest", said, "Into every gap he put his illusion, his halt, which he calls God. The concept, Although not the exact term, it goes back to Henry Drummond, a 19th-century evangelical lecturer, in his Lowell Lectures on the Ascent of Man of 1893. He chastises Christians who point to things that science cannot explain is not—"the gap they will fill with God" and urges them to embrace all nature as God, "an immanent God, who is the God of evolution, compared to the occasional wonder worker I am infinitely grand, the deity of an older theology.

Name of God in Buddhism

Buddhism is a religion that does not include a belief in a creator deity, or any eternal divine personality. Dev Brahma Sahampati asks Buddha to teach. Buddhism accepts the existence of devas (celestial beings, literally "shining ones"), but these beings are not creator gods, nor are they eternal (they suffer and go). Buddhist teachings state that devas (sometimes translated as deities) and other Buddhist deities, heavens and rebirths are called samsara, or the doctrine of cyclic rebirth. Buddhism teaches that none of these deities is a creator or eternal being, although they may live very long lives. In Buddhism, deities also get caught in the cycle of rebirth and are not necessarily virtuous. Thus, while Buddhism includes many deities, its main focus is not on them. Peter Howen calls this "trans-polytheism". 34 Buddhist texts also state that worldly deities such as Mahabrahma are misunderstood as creators. Buddhist ontology follows the principle of dependent origination, whereby all events arise in dependence on other events, so

No primitive motionless mover can be accepted or recognized. Gautama Buddha is also shown in early Buddhist texts as saying that he did not see a single beginning of the universe. Buddha has told how the universe was created in the Brahma-Jala Suta. Creation and destruction of the universe happen again and again. God or Mahabrahma does not create the universe because the world runs on the principle of Pratityasamutpada i.e. Karkaran-Bhav. According to Lord Buddha, Karma is responsible for the sorrows and happiness of human beings, not God or Mahabrahma. But elsewhere the Buddha has called the Supreme Truth indescribable.

Name of God in Taoism

The word "Tao" (i) has several meanings in both ancient and modern Chinese. In addition to the purely professional use of meaning road, channel, path, principle, or similar, the word has acquired a variety of different and often confusing metaphorical, philosophical, and religious uses. In most belief systems, the term is used symbolically in the sense of "the way" as the right or proper way of existence, or in reference to ongoing practices of attainment or coming into complete existence, or enlightenment or It is done with reference to the spiritual condition. Perfection which is the result of such practices. Some scholars make a sharp distinction between the ethical or moral use of the word "Tao" that is prominent in Confucianism and religious Taoism and the more spiritual use of the word used in philosophical Taoism and most forms of Mahayana Buddhism; Others maintain that these are not separate uses or meanings, viewing them as mutually inclusive and compatible approaches to defining the doctrine. The original use of the term was as a form of practice rather than doctrine. A term used as a convention that cannot otherwise be discussed in words and in early writings such as the Tao Te Ching and the I ching pain tao sometimes "named tao"

refers to the Tao) and the Tao itself ("the nameless Tao"), which cannot be expressed or understood in language. Liu Da claims that the Tao is properly understood as an experiential and evolving concept and that there are not only cultural and religious differences in the interpretation of the Tao but individual differences that reflect the character of individual practitioners.

Name of God In Confucianism

the god name tian (风) is one of the oldest Chinese words for heaven and is an important concept in Chinese mythology, philosophy and religion. During the Shang dynasty (17th–11th centuries BCE), the Chinese referred to their supreme deity as Shangdi (+ , "Lord on High") or Dou (, "Lord"). During the following Zhou dynasty, tian became synonymous with the figure.

Heaven worship was an orthodox state religion of China before the 20th century.

The belief based on the philosophical, social and political ideas of Confucius is named Confucianism or Kungfutsianism. According to Confucius, goodness is the natural quality of man. Man has got this natural quality from God. Therefore, to act according to this nature is to respect the will of God and not to act according to it is to disobey God.

Reference– Ishwar Kalpana in different religions, Bihar Hindi Granth Academy.

My another books

Sr no.	Book
1	World's Major religions, doctrines and sects
2	An introduction to the Holy Qur'an and it's unsolved mysteries
3	How did humans and language originate ?
4	Islam an introduction and sect
5	Sermons of great people
6	Prayer
7	Allah an introduction
8	Is Al khizr still alive today?
9	Story of harut and marut
10	Grief
11	The mysterious story of Al kahf (Ar raqim)
12	Naming of God
13	Who was Sheeba?
14	Death concept of the Holy Quran

15	What is soul? In view of Religion and science
16	Real Alexander Zulqurnain
17	Where is peace?
18	Origin of ancient religious book, it's author and original copy
19	An introduction to the bible and is the original bible still available today?
20	Does a parallel universe exist?
21	Promise to your self or God?
22	Evidence of God existance
23	Prediction of holy Quran
24	Humanity in the holy Quran?
25	Commandnends of the holy Quran, right or wrong?
26	Similarity in the world famous holy books
27	Is Zulkifl the same Gautam Buddha?
28	Adam to Muhammad
29	Why isolated?

30	For Divorce! Who is responsible?
31	Hadith to denomination
32	Karma is the best?
33	According to dreams, religion Science
34	End day

<u>All these books are available in Hindi</u> language and other international languages and are also available in e-book for <u>free on Google Play Store</u>.

<u>All the books are available in paper back edition and hard cover edition as well.</u>
<u>These books are also available on Amazon,Flipkart and notionpress.com.</u>

My personal introduction

My Personal Introduction My name is Abdul Waheed, my father's name is Late Haji Ubaidur Rahman and mother's name is Jaibunnisa. I have liked scientific ideology since childhood and have a calm nature and attachment to books. Due to which my curiosity interest has been continuously used in new discoveries and information. I got selected in polytechnic while doing BSc, but unfortunately it remained incomplete because father and brother died.

<u>Two words of my father, which are very precious for my life,</u>
<u>first - earn honestly, do not take support of lies.</u>
<u>secondly, respect food and eat as much as you want.</u>

That's why the education remained incomplete due to the responsibility of the house, then later getting married. Still did not lose courage and today the book is available in front of you in the form of my thoughts. If any information is left incomplete, please let us know.

Thank you .- Abdul Waheed, Barabanki, Uttar Pradesh, INDIA.

Contact-

Abdul Waheed, Barabanki, Uttar pradesh, India

https,https://www.facebook.com/profile.php?id=100091298026218